SKATEBOARD SAVE

BY JAKE MADDOX

illustrated by Sean Tiffany

text by Eric Stevens

Librarian Reviewer
Chris Kreie
Media Specialist, Eden Prairie Schools, MN
MS in Information Media, St. Cloud State University, MN

Reading Consultant
Mary Evenson
Middle School Teacher, Edina Public Schools, MN
MA in Education, University of Minnesota

W9-BFD-802

STONE ARCH BOOKS
www.stonearchbooks.com

Impact Books are published by Stone Arch Books
A Capstone Imprint
151 Good Counsel Drive, P.O. Box 669
Mankato, Minnesota 56002
www.capstonepub.com

Copyright © 2009 by Stone Arch Books

Library of Congress Cataloging-in-Publication Data
Maddox, Jake.
    Skateboard Save / by Jake Maddox; illustrated by Sean Tiffany.
    p. cm. — (Impact Books. A Jake Maddox Sports Story)
    ISBN 978-1-4342-0775-3 (library binding)
    ISBN 978-1-4342-0871-2 (pbk.)
    [1. Skateboarding—Fiction. 2. Sportsmanship—Fiction.] I. Tiffany,
Sean, ill. II. Title.
PZ7.M25643Skd 2009
[Fic]—dc22   2008004294

Summary: When Riley enters the skateboarding contest, he doesn't
expect to help his biggest rival.

Art Director: Heather Kindseth
Graphic Designer: Kay Fraser

Printed in the United States of America in Stevens Point, Wisconsin.
102009
005625R

TABLE OF CONTENTS

CHAPTER 1

Ready to Roll 5

CHAPTER 2

Reputation 12

CHAPTER 3

The Contest. 17

CHAPTER 4

VIPs 23

CHAPTER 5

Bullies Are Back 28

CHAPTER 6

A Threat. 33

CHAPTER 7

The Big Day 38

CHAPTER 8

Round Two 46

CHAPTER 9

Final Round 51

CHAPTER 10

The Champion 59

CHAPTER 1
READY TO ROLL

Riley Alexander looked down into the half-pipe. His skateboard hung over the edge, ready to roll.

It was a typical Wednesday afternoon. School had been kind of boring, but going to the skate park always made Riley feel better. Just placing his foot on the skateboard's deck filled him with energy.

Riley took a deep breath. Then he dropped into the pipe.

He had been skating that half-pipe since he was nine. Now, five years later, he was an expert.

By the time he reached the other edge, Riley had enough speed for a kickflip. For an instant, he was completely airborne. With one hand, he held his board against his feet.

He did a few more tricks. Then he glided to the bottom.

Finally, he headed back to the top of the pipe to go again. But as he steadied himself before dropping in, someone grabbed his shoulder.

Riley spun around.

Three seniors from Riley's school were standing there. "Nice board, kid," one of them said. "Mind if I test it out?"

"Yeah, I do!" Riley snapped. But the other two boys stepped up and pushed him down.

The older guys laughed. "Take it easy," the first guy said as he grabbed the board from Riley. "I'm not going to break it."

The other guys held Riley on the ground as their friend spun the skateboard in his hands. Riley had a bad feeling that breaking the board was exactly what they planned to do.

"What are you doing?" Riley yelled as the bully stepped onto his board.

"I'm just having a little fun!" the guy called as he slid hard along a cement bench.

Riley pictured the bully taking the slide too hard and cracking the board.

"You better not break my board!" Riley called out.

One of the guys told him to be quiet. Riley struggled to get up. "Give it back!" he called out.

As the leader of the guys was about to go for another rough slide, a voice shouted out from behind the half-pipe. "Hey, knock it off," the voice said.

The three bullies looked up. The one on the board came to a stop and kicked the board into his hand.

"What gives?" the bully said. He looked confused as Bernie Chu, also a senior and one of the best skaters in Riverton, stepped out from the shadows.

Riley swallowed hard. He'd seen Bernie around school.

Bernie was a tough kid. He was always giving younger kids — and even some of the other seniors — a hard time.

"We were just fooling around," said the bully with Riley's board.

"Enough," Bernie snapped. He took Riley's board from the bully. "Get out of here," he added.

The three bullies looked confused. "What?" their leader said. "Bernie, you do this stuff to these little skaters all the time. What's your problem today?"

Bernie just growled. The three bullies glanced at each other. "Whatever," their leader said. Then they turned and walked out of the skate park.

Riley got to his feet. Bernie dropped the board on its wheels and slid it over to him.

Riley stopped it with his foot. Then he kicked the board into his hand.

"Thanks," Riley said. But Bernie didn't even look at him. He just turned around and walked off.

CHAPTER 2
REPUTATION

"It's true, Jay," Riley said the next day as he chewed a huge bite of his sandwich. "Bernie Chu saved my board."

His best friend, Jay, pointed over at the lunch line. "That Bernie Chu?" he asked.

Riley turned around and saw Bernie Chu walking away from the lunch line. He was carrying a full tray and elbowing people out of his way. "Move it," he grunted at one kid.

The kid stumbled, dropped his tray, slipped on some gravy, and fell face-first onto his own mashed potatoes. The whole cafeteria burst into laughter.

Riley turned back to Jay. "Yup. That Bernie Chu," Riley said.

"I don't believe it," Jay said, tearing open a ketchup packet and squirting it all over his fries. "Maybe you should go thank him," he added with a smirk.

"If I do go talk to him," Riley replied, "will you believe me?"

"I do believe you," Jay said quickly. "But you should still thank him. I mean, it's a good idea to be polite to a guy whose left leg is bigger than your whole body."

Riley stood up. "Fine," he said. "I'll go thank him."

He headed to the table on the edge of the room. That was where Bernie always ate by himself.

"Um, Bernie?" Riley said as he reached the senior's table.

Bernie was taking a long drink of milk. He glanced at Riley over the carton as he continued to drink.

"I just wanted to say thanks for saving my skateboard yesterday," Riley went on.

Bernie put down his milk and crushed the carton with his palm. "Go away," Bernie said through his teeth.

Riley didn't have to be told twice. He backed away slowly, turned around, and walked over to his own table. Jay was barely holding in his laughter as Riley sat down.

"That was awesome," Jay said.

"I don't get it," Riley said. "Why is he acting like that?"

"That's obvious!" Jay said, pushing his empty tray away. "Bernie couldn't let the whole school know that he'd been nice to you. It would ruin his reputation."

Is that the truth? Riley wondered. *Is Bernie Chu really just worried about his reputation?*

CHAPTER 3
THE CONTEST

After school that day, Riley and Jay walked home past the skate park.

"I wish they'd let us bring our boards to school," Riley said, glancing over at the half-pipe. "It's stupid to walk all the way home to get my board and then come back here to practice."

Jay nodded. "Hey, check that out!" he said, pointing toward the fence that circled the park.

Two men wearing green overalls were up on ladders, hanging a big banner from the top of the fence. The banner read, "First Annual Skateboarding Contest."

"Let's go check it out," Riley said.

There was a smaller sign on a wall. It read:

SKATEBOARDING
CONTEST
THIS SATURDAY!

No One Over 17 Years Old Allowed
Park Open Only For Competitors
To Practice Till Saturday

SIGN UP IN PARK OFFICE

"Cool!" Jay said. "You have to enter, Riley!"

Riley nodded. "I will if you do," he said. "It does sound pretty cool."

Jay shrugged. "All right," he replied, "but I'm pretty nervous about it."

The boys walked over to the office. "We're here to sign up," Jay said when they walked in.

"Great!" said the woman at the counter. She held up a clipboard. "Put your names on this list."

Riley and Jay filled in their names and handed the clipboard back.

"All right, Riley and Jay," the woman said after reading their names. "I'm Lizzie, and I'll be one of the judges on Saturday. Nice to meet you."

Riley and Jay smiled at her.

"Each of you gets one of these buttons," Lizzie went on.

She handed them two buttons. The buttons were bright blue and read, "Skateboard Competition."

"Wear them on your shirts whenever you come to the park between now and Saturday," she explained. "You'll need them to get in the park to practice."

"Thanks, Lizzie," Jay said. They headed out of the office.

"This is going to be awesome," Riley said. He pinned his button on his shirt.

"I guess," said Jay, fumbling with his own button. "I've never been in a competition before, though. So I guess I'm kind of nervous."

"I haven't been in one either," Riley replied. "But everyone knows we're two of the best around here."

"Not as good as Bernie, though," Jay pointed out.

"And don't forget that kid who grabbed my board yesterday," Riley added. "That kid was good, even if he was a jerk."

CHAPTER 4

VIPs

After Jay and Riley stopped at their houses and grabbed their boards, they headed back to the park.

Lizzie was hanging around near the park entrance when they arrived. She glanced at them, noticed their buttons, and smiled.

"Come on in, guys," she said. "Competitors only!"

"This is pretty cool," Riley said.

"Yeah," Jay replied. "We're VIPs."

The park was busier than usual, for a weekday afternoon. Skaters with buttons on their shirts were lining up for the half-pipe. The other course, the street course, was empty, except for three kids.

Jay pointed at the three kids. "Are those the guys who took your board yesterday?" he asked.

"Yup," Riley replied. "Let's stay out of their sight."

Jay nodded. "I want to practice on the half-pipe anyway," he said. "Let them have the street course."

Riley and Jay headed over to the pipe. They stopped at the end of the line.

"This is weird," Riley said. "A line at the skate park on a Thursday."

After they waited for ten minutes, it was finally their turn. They climbed to the edge. But before they could drop, someone else sped past them and dropped in.

"Whoa, buddy!" Jay shouted. "Watch it."

The skater didn't seem to hear him, though. He just kept right on skating.

Riley and Jay watched as the guy flew back and forth and up and down in the pipe. After a moment, the skater did a nice kickflip off the far edge of the half-pipe.

Then he seemed to pause in midair. Riley and Jay could see his face clearly

"It's Bernie!" Riley said. "He must be practicing for the competition."

"You mean he's not over seventeen?" Jay asked.

Riley shrugged. "Guess not," he said.

They watched Bernie finish his turn on the pipe. Then he left the park.

Since the line behind them was growing longer, Riley and Jay took their turns quickly. Riley only had time to try out a few new tricks.

Jay glanced at his watch. "It's four already," he said. "I'm late."

"Guitar lessons?" Riley asked.

Jay nodded. "I'm always late," he said.

Riley laughed. "Well, I'm going to stay and get in as many runs as I can before dinner," he said. "I want to get my handplant perfect for Saturday."

"If you can pull that off, you'll win for sure!" Jay said.

CHAPTER 5
BULLIES ARE BACK

After school the next day, Riley waited for Jay out front, like he did every day. It had rained all day, but the sun was finally starting to peek from behind the gray clouds. Riley was excited to get to the skate park to start practicing.

"Hey, kid," a voice called out. Riley turned to look. Bernie was standing by the bike rack. The three skate park bullies were behind him.

Uh-oh, Riley thought. But he stood where he was and called back, "What's up, Bernie?"

"Are you Riley something?" Bernie asked, walking up to him.

Bernie was about a foot taller than Riley, and maybe twice as wide. Riley looked up at him. "Yes. I'm Riley Alexander," he replied.

Bernie growled a little. "My friends here tell me you're entering the competition on Saturday," he said. "That true?"

Riley nodded. "Yeah," he said.

"My friends also tell me you think you're some kind of hotshot," Bernie added. "They say that after I left the park yesterday, you tried a handplant a few times."

Riley swallowed hard.

"Is that true?" Bernie added, poking Riley in the chest with his forefinger.

"Yes, that's true too," Riley replied.

Bernie threw his head back and laughed. "Are you crazy?" he asked. "You can't pull that trick off, and you know it!"

Bernie's smile went away. He leaned over. Riley could feel Bernie's breath on his face. It smelled like hot dogs.

"You can't win, kid," Bernie said quietly. "So on Saturday, if you know what's good for you, don't show up."

Riley didn't know what to say. He just stared back at Bernie's face.

Suddenly Bernie put his hand on Riley's chest and pushed him. He didn't push hard, but the ground was slippery. Riley fell and landed in a puddle of mud.

Bernie looked down at Riley with a blank look on his face. The three bullies behind Bernie cracked up laughing.

"Good one, Bernie," one of them said.

Still laughing, the three guys followed Bernie as he turned and walked away. Riley sat there, watching them leave, feeling the muddy water soaking into his jeans.

CHAPTER 6
A THREAT

"I'd say that was a threat," Jay said.

Riley had gone home to change his jeans and grab his board. Now he and Jay were sitting on the edge of the half-pipe at the skate park. They were taking a break from practicing and were watching some of the other competitors.

"I don't get it," Riley said, shaking his head. "He was nice to me the other day, and then he pushed me in the mud today."

"Who knows why he'd do that," Jay replied. "He must be worried that you're going to beat him."

"What gives you that idea?" Riley asked.

"Why else would he want you to drop out of the competition?" Jay replied. "He must think you have a shot. It's the only possible reason."

"Maybe," Riley muttered.

"Maybe?" Jay said, laughing. "You're better than all these skaters. You're totally a threat to Bernie's chances."

Riley thought for a moment. He watched a girl from a different high school try a rock and roll. She lost it and ended up sliding on her belly to the bottom of the pipe. A few of the kids on the edge clapped or laughed.

"See?" Jay said.

"Fine, I guess I'm better than she is," Riley said.

"Yeah, you are. And you're better than everybody else here!" Jay said.

"Maybe," Riley agreed, "but what about what Bernie said?"

"What do you mean? The threat?" Jay asked.

"Yeah, the threat," Riley replied, sounding worried. "He said not to show up if I know what's good for me! What am I supposed to do?"

"He won't do anything," Jay said. "He's just trying to scare you."

"Well, he's doing a good job of it," Riley replied.

"All he did was get your pants muddy," Jay said. "Big deal. You have to stay in the competition."

"Hmm. If you say so," said Riley.

He wasn't so sure staying in the competition was a good idea, especially if he might actually beat Bernie.

CHAPTER 7
THE BIG DAY

On Saturday morning, Riley met Jay on the way to the park. Both boys were skating slowly down the street as the sun rose higher in the sky. Jay was eating an apple, and Riley was carrying his backpack.

"You ready?" Jay said to Riley as he skated next to his friend.

"I guess so," Riley replied.

"What's in the bag?" Jay asked, nodding at Riley's backpack.

"Just my board repair tool kit," Riley replied. "You never know."

Soon they were rolling up to the park gate.

"Wow," Jay said. "I've never seen the park like this before."

Skaters were everywhere. At the half-pipe, a bunch of kids were waiting for their turns while one skater did tricks like spins, inverts, and double turns.

"Whoa, did you see that?" Jay asked.

Riley nodded. He said, "A double turn. I guess I don't have a chance after all."

The awesome skater did a couple more tricks and then stepped off the board.

"This guy's amazing," Jay said. "Well, at least you can take second."

Riley nodded. Then the skater's helmet came off. "That's not a guy. It's Lizzie!" he said with a laugh.

"Cool!" said Jay. "But she's a judge, so you're still the best in the competition."

"Okay, guys," Lizzie announced from the half-pipe platform. "Thanks to everyone for showing up for the park's first competition."

Everyone gathered around the half-pipe. Riley spotted Bernie and his bully friends pushing their way to the front of the pack.

"We're going to get the first round started right away," Lizzie went on. "This is going to be a quick round. And I'll be the only judge. When you finish, I'll give you a thumbs-up or a thumbs-down to let you know if you'll be skating in the second round."

The skaters realized some of them would be out in just a few minutes. There was some muttering in the crowd.

"Line up and get ready to show me something awesome," Lizzie said.

Soon, music was blasting. A line of one hundred skaters was forming.

Riley dropped his backpack off in Lizzie's office. Then he and Jay got in line.

"I can't even see the half-pipe from here," Jay said, stretching his neck.

"But there's Lizzie," Riley said, pointing to the head judge standing at the side of the half-pipe. "I can see whether people are getting thumbs-up or down, at least."

Jay couldn't see Lizzie, so as each skater came off the pipe, Riley told Jay how the judging was going.

"There's a thumbs-down, and another," he said. "Oooh, there's a thumbs-up."

The skater who'd gotten the thumbs-up pulled off his helmet. "It's Bernie!" Riley said.

Jay shook his head. "Who else?" he said.

After about twenty minutes of waiting, it was Jay's turn. He did a perfect spin to fakie drop in, and a few clean kickflips and ollies before gliding out of the pipe. Lizzie gave him a thumbs-up.

Riley called out, "Nice one, Jay!"

Then the whistle blew again. It was Riley's turn.

He dropped in straight and crouched to get some speed. His first time up the vert, he got pretty good air and landed fakie.

Up the other side, he pulled off a spin. On his last pass, he rock and rolled into fakie and then glided out. Lizzie gave him a thumbs-up.

Jay was at the edge of the ramp. He gave him a high five. "Nice one, Riley!" he said. "You hear the applause you got for that spin?"

Riley nodded. "That was a pretty good run!" he said.

"Now the real skating starts," said Jay. "Come on. All of the skaters who got thumbs-up are by the street course."

Jay and Riley walked over. About ten other skaters were there. Riley recognized a few from school, including Bernie Chu.

"Hey, kid," Bernie said. "It's not too late for you to go home."

The other skaters looked at Riley. He felt himself turning red.

Riley and Jay sat on a cement bench. "Why won't he leave me alone?" Riley said.

"He's just messing with you," Jay said. "He's trying to make you look stupid in front of the other skaters, so you'll quit."

Riley shook his head. "No way can I quit now," he said.

CHAPTER 8
ROUND TWO

Only twenty skaters made it into round two. Most of the kids who were cut from round one stuck around to watch.

Jay was the first skater. He dropped straight, took one turn to pick up speed, and then attempted a turn on the way back. But he blew it and slid on his kneepads to the bottom of the pipe.

Oh no, thought Riley. Then Jay's score came up. It was 7.7.

A few other skaters took their turns, but most of them scored over 8. Jay wasn't making it to round three.

Then it was Bernie Chu's turn. He dropped in and got amazing speed. Over Bernie's next three passes, he just kept getting more and more air.

"Higher! Higher!" the crowd called out. And Bernie did get higher. Riley had never seen a skater get air like that before.

Finally, Bernie pulled off a perfect double turn, landing on his feet and standing. He caught his board on the other side.

Bernie dropped in and glided off the ramp. After a few moments, his score came up.

Riley couldn't believe it. Bernie Chu had scored 9.9!

"That's going to be hard to beat," Jay said.

Riley nodded. *It's going to be impossible*, he thought.

Soon it was Riley's turn. He dropped straight in and crouched for speed, got some good air, and had nice speed on the way back.

I have to go for it, he thought. *The handplant.*

He reached the edge of the half-pipe and grabbed it, kicked his feet over his head, and held on to his board. When he landed it clean, he heard the crowd going wild.

He caught his board at the top of the ramp and pumped his fist.

"Woo!" Jay called out from the side of the ramp. "Go, Riley! Nice run!"

Riley watched for the judges to hold up his score. Soon Lizzie held up a card: 9.7!

After all the skaters had finished round two, the judges whispered to each other. None of the skaters had scored above 8.8 except Riley and Bernie.

Finally, Lizzie stood up and called out, "Stick around for round three! This will be the final round to decide who wins the first competition at Riverton Skate Park. Riley Alexander versus Bernie Chu!"

CHAPTER 9
FINAL ROUND

While the competition broke for lunch, Riley and Bernie were sitting in the office with Lizzie. She'd given each of them a burger and a bottle of juice.

Bernie ate his burger in two bites. Then he just sat there frowning.

"Okay, guys," Lizzie said. "Here's how it's going to work in round three."

Riley swallowed hard as he watched Bernie.

He thought back to Wednesday night, when Bernie had saved his board from those three bullies. But then he'd been mean the very next day.

Maybe Jay was right, Riley thought. *Maybe Bernie's just worried about his reputation.*

"In the third round," Lizzie went on, "you'll each have three runs. Your total score will be out of thirty points — ten for each run. The best score after three runs wins. Got it?"

Riley nodded. Bernie grunted.

"Okay then," said Lizzie, getting to her feet. "We'll get started when you're both ready."

Jay was waiting for Riley outside the office. "See?" he said. "I told you you're better than the other skaters here!"

"Except Bernie," Riley said. "He beat me in round two."

Jay shrugged. "He got lucky with that double turn," he said. "I bet he won't even try it again."

A few minutes later, Riley sat on the edge of the half-pipe. Bernie got ready to start his run.

Lizzie stood next to Bernie with her megaphone. "Okay, guys," she announced. "First up, coming into the final round with a 9.9 and a sweet double turn in round two, here's Bernie Chu."

Bernie dropped in. His run looked as good as his round two run. Riley was impressed by his air, his inverts, everything. It was perfect. And sure enough, the judges held up a 9.9 again.

Riley felt nervous as he got set to drop in for his first go. But the drop in felt good, and he had great speed. He pulled off his handplant again, but he didn't hold it long enough. Then the best aerial he could pull off was spinning once in the air. It was nothing compared to Bernie's run.

The judges held up his score: 9.1.

Riley heard Jay cheering. "Nice run, Riley," he called out. But Riley knew he'd have to pick it up in his second run to compete with Bernie.

Bernie dropped in for his second run. Lizzie called out, "Here comes Chu for his second go in this final round."

He picked up speed. "Nice air there," Lizzie announced. "Whoa! Dark disaster, nice one, Chu!"

Riley swallowed hard. Bernie was doing some pretty hard moves.

When Bernie caught his board at the top of the ramp and the whistle blew, Riley was really worried.

Then the judges held up Bernie's score. Another 9.9!

"Beat that," Bernie said, looking down at Riley.

I don't think I can, Riley thought. He took a deep breath and dropped in.

"Here goes Riley Alexander," Lizzie said to the crowd. "He's getting some good air. And here's the handplant. Nice landing, but a little shaky maybe."

Riley took two passes to get some speed and some air.

"He's got something planned, I think," Lizzie called out. "Here it comes. A double turn! Can he do it?"

Riley finished the double turn and eyed the ramp. But his board was slipping forward.

Riley found himself sliding on his butt to the bottom of the ramp. His board came to a stop beside him.

"He missed the landing," Lizzie announced. "Let's see if he can save this run."

Riley got up. He glided back and forth for some speed. He got up enough to pull off another trick before the whistle. But he knew it wasn't enough to beat Bernie's 9.9s.

Lizzie held up Riley's score: 8.9. A full point behind Bernie.

"To win, I'll have to gain almost two full points on Bernie," Riley complained to Jay as the two waited for Bernie's third run. "It's impossible!"

"Maybe not," Jay said, pointing to Bernie, on the other side of the ramp. "Look!"

Riley glanced up at Bernie. He was fiddling with the rear truck of his board, which was wobbling a lot.

"Looks like his board is busted," Jay said. "He won't be able to take his third run!"

Riley was shocked. "That trick must have knocked a screw loose or something," he whispered.

"He's going to have to forfeit," Jay said with a huge grin, "and you'll win!"

CHAPTER 10
THE CHAMPION

Riley shook his head. "That's not how I want to win," he said. "Wait here a second."

Riley got up. Then he skated right over to Lizzie's office.

He stepped inside and found his backpack. Then he hustled back to where Bernie was coming down the steps.

"Let me take a look," Riley said, reaching into his backpack for some tools.

Bernie looked surprised, but he handed Riley the board.

"Looks like you lost a bolt doing that dark disaster," Riley said. "Which was pretty sweet, by the way."

Bernie frowned. "Thanks," he said.

After a minute, Riley held up the board again. "Should be okay now," he said. "You should really learn a little about board repairs."

"Right," Bernie grunted. "Thanks." Riley just smiled and walked off.

"I don't get you at all, dude," Jay said as Riley sat down next to him. "There's no way you can win now!"

Riley shrugged. "He saved my board once," he said. "Now I've saved his board once."

Jay just shook his head. They watched as Bernie dropped in.

"You know if he does better than an 8, you can't win," Jay pointed out.

"I know," replied Riley.

Bernie had another great run. Two handplants later, he caught his board and stopped next to Jay and Riley right at the whistle.

Riley held up his hand for a high five. Bernie slapped his hand and smiled.

Lizzie and the other judges whispered to each other for a few minutes. Then Lizzie held up a score card: 9.8.

"Bernie Chu is the first champion of Riverton Skate Park!" Lizzie announced over the megaphone.

All of the skaters went wild cheering for Bernie.

"And in second place," Lizzie went on, "with a great show for anyone, especially for a guy who's only fourteen, Riley Alexander!" Riley beamed as everyone in the park cheered for him, too.

During all the cheering, Bernie turned to Riley and held out his hand. Riley shook it.

"Thanks for saving my board," Bernie said.

"You did the same for me," Riley said.

"You're a really good skater," Bernie said. "I'm glad I saved your board the other day, kid — I mean, Riley."

Riley smiled. In the rest of the park, the skaters and judges continued to clap and cheer.

ABOUT THE AUTHOR

Eric Stevens lives in St. Paul, Minnesota. He is studying to become a middle-school English teacher. Some of his favorite things include pizza, playing video games, watching cooking shows on TV, riding his bike, and trying new restaurants. Some of his least favorite things include olives and shoveling snow.

ABOUT THE ILLUSTRATOR

When Sean Tiffany was growing up, he lived on a small island off the coast of Maine. Every day, from sixth grade until he graduated from high school, he had to take a boat to get to school. When Sean isn't working on his art, he works on a multimedia project called "OilCan Drive," which combines music and art. He has a pet cactus named Jim.

GLOSSARY

airborne (AIR-born)—in the air

annual (ANN-yoo-uhl)—if something is annual, it happens every year

competition (kom-puh-TISH-uhn)—a contest

competitors (kuhm-PET-i-turz)—the people participating in a contest

expert (EK-spurt)—someone who is very skilled at something

forfeit (FOR-fit)—give up

hotshot (HOT-shot)—a show-off

megaphone (MEG-uh-fone)—a device that is used to make a voice sound louder

reputation (rep-yuh-TAY-shuhn)—what other people think about you

ruin (ROO-in)—to spoil or destroy something

tough (TUHF)—difficult to deal with

VIP (VEE EYE PEE)—short for Very Important Person

SKATEBOARD WORDS

- **aerial** (AYR-ee-uhl)—a trick done in the air.

- **air** (AYR)—riding with all four wheels off the ground

- **dark disaster** (DARK duh-ZASS-tur)—an advanced trick, in which the skater performs a half-flip and lands on the rim of the ramp in the center of the skateboard, with the front wheels facing down the ramp

- **deck** (DEK)—the board part of the skateboard

- **drop in** (DROP IN)—enter the ramp to start a run

- **fakie** (FAY-kee)—riding the board backward

- **half-pipe** (HAF PIPE)—a U-shaped ramp with a flat section in the middle

YOU SHOULD KNOW

- **handplant** (HAND-plant)—a form of handstand, where the board is held in the air by hands or feet

- **invert** (IN-vurt)—a handplant

- **kickflip** (KIK-flip)—during an ollie, a kickflip is performed by pushing down on the board with the toes, causing the board to flip over

- **ollie** (OLL-lee)—a jump performed by tapping the back of the board on the ground

- **rock and roll** (ROK AND ROLL)—a trick in which the bottom of the board is tapped on the rim of the ramp before a kickflip, then reentering the ramp

- **run** (RUN)—a turn on the half-pipe

- **vert** (VURT)—another name for the half-pipe

DISCUSSION QUESTIONS

1. After Bernie pushed him in the mud, Riley just sat there. What would you have done? What would have been the best thing to do?

2. How do you think Jay felt when Riley made it to the final round but he didn't?

3. Jay told Riley that Bernie was worried about his reputation. What do you think Jay meant?

WRITING PROMPTS

1. Bernie won the competition. How would Riley have felt if he won? Write a paragraph describing how he would feel if he had won the competition.

2. Sometimes it can be interesting to think about a situation from another person's point of view. Try writing chapter 10 (on page 59) from Bernie's point of view. What does he think about? How does he feel?

3. Did you learn new skateboarding words when you read this book? Write a paragraph that uses three new words that you learned from this book.

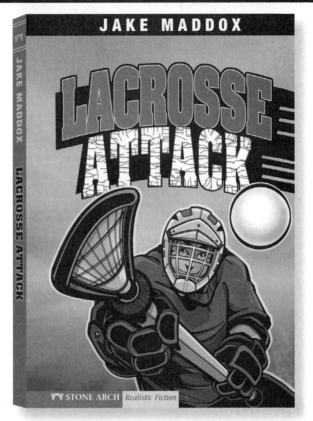

JAKE MADDOX

LACROSSE ATTACK

JAKE MADDOX

LACROSSE ATTACK

STONE ARCH *Realistic Fiction*

Peter made the varsity lacrosse team. But Hurley Johnson, the team's captain, doesn't want Peter to take his position. He'll stop at nothing to make Peter quit. Will Peter give up, or can he prove he deserves to be on the team?

BY JAKE MADDOX

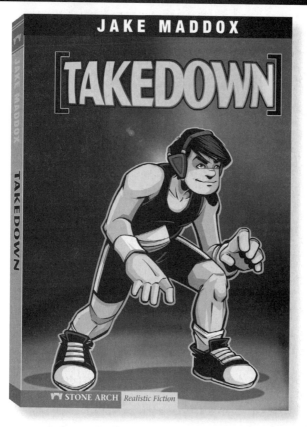

JAKE MADDOX

[TAKEDOWN]

JAKE MADDOX

TAKEDOWN

STONE ARCH *Realistic Fiction*

Jeff can't control his temper. One day, he meets
Logan, one of the captains of his school's
wrestling team. Once Jeff learns about wrestling,
he knows he can be good at it. But can he
control his anger long enough to win a match?

INTERNET SITES

Do you want to know more about subjects related to this book? Or are you interested in learning about other topics? Then check out FactHound, a fun, easy way to find Internet sites.

Our investigative staff has already sniffed out great sites for you!

Here's how to use FactHound:

1. Visit *www.facthound.com*

2. Select your grade level.

3. To learn more about subjects related to this book, type in the book's ISBN number: **9781434207753**.

4. Click the **Fetch It** button.

FactHound will fetch the best Internet sites for you!